Hope
for Joy

Written by
Sarah Miner
Illustrated by
Sara Lynn Sanders
*for the Hope Institute
of Uganda*

Printed in the United States of America
ISBN 978-0-9963243-0-4

Book Designer: Sarah Miner

The Hope Institute of Uganda
1260 Milton Avenue
Janesville, WI 53546

www.hopeinstituteuganda.org

Dedicated to Ellen Joy Willis (1965-2011) whose life was taken from us by breast cancer. Ellen was devoted to ending poverty in Africa. May this book be a tribute to her tireless effort.

Table of Contents

Foreword

I saw their faces. I experienced their smiles. I remember their stories—that is why I keep selling Jinja Jewelry beads for the Hope Institute of Uganda. It has been an honor to partner with Joy and Gideon Ngobi who have made it their mission to bring help and hope to people living in poverty in their homeland.

I first met Joy at Sky Lodge Family Camp in Wisconsin. Her joyful spirit and the beads she brought to sell captured my attention. To think that such beauty could come from discarded paper was fascinating to me. When I learned that Joy was selling the jewelry for women in Uganda so they could take care of their families and send their children to school, I was eager to help.

I began selling Jinja Jewelry in 2010. One month later, I started a fair trade business in Greenville, IL called Roots-n-Streams (Gifts With Purpose). Getting to know Joy and traveling with her to Uganda to meet the bead makers has been one of the most rewarding experiences in my life. It has been a delight to share pictures and stories with others when I go out to sell in a variety of locations and speak to groups of all ages. Having this beautifully illustrated book, with a story that touches your heart, inspires me to keep making connections and sharing with others. As you read, may you be encouraged to consider how recycled paper and a simple sale can change a life.

Kim Brannon
Roots-n-Streams (Gifts With Purpose), Director
Greenville Free Methodist Church – Greenville, IL

Hope
for **Joy**

Hi! My name is Joy. I just love my name because when I hear Mama say my name, it makes me happy. I think my name makes Mama happy, too. She smiles most of the time when she says my name. Mama is always very busy because I have five brothers and three sisters so it makes me happy when she smiles.

My story starts on a hot afternoon in my small village outside of Jinja, Uganda. I watched my mother string beads on a piece of wire. Mama sat under a tree on the hard dirt ground finishing a new bracelet. She made the beads last week, and they looked like glass, but I knew they were nothing more than strips of paper from magazines rolled together. Mama made the bracelets for the Hope Institute and other women did, too. The women worked together each day, and I was happy Mama could make her jewelry at home and be with my siblings and me.

I watched as Mama tied the final knot, and the two-week process was completed. For me, the way my mother made the beads was like magic! I never tired of watching her cut strips of paper over and over, glue them together, hang and dry them, and finally apply a clear coating to make the bead a finished bracelet. I never got over how unique and beautiful each bead and bracelet was. No two were the same! It's so fun to watch Mama make her bracelets that some days I don't even play with my friends.

As I sat with Mama, a weird sound suddenly caught my attention. I stood up and stepped into the blazing hot, tropical sun to get a better look at what was happening.

"Mama, who are they?" I asked, pointing at the people making the weird sound. A group of white people walked down the road, holding funny looking things in their hands. They were dressed so different from us.

Mama stood up and walked over to me.

"They are bazungu visiting from America, Joy," Mama said, using the native word for white people. "They are vol-unteers."

"Bazungu from America?" I asked. I wondered what exactly they were doing in my village because I had never seen anybody that didn't look like my family or me.

"They volunteer for the Hope Institute of Uganda," Mama continued. "You know. The people I make the bracelets for."

I knew what the Hope Institute of Uganda was because my mother and sister had told me all about it. The people who volunteer for them are from a country very far from us named America. Mama said Americans looked like the people I was watching. They bought the beaded jewelry

Mama makes and not only love the beautiful jewelry, but also love being able to help children in my country go to school. Since people in America buy Mama's jewelry, my older sister, Sarah, is able to go to school. I wish I could go to school, but it's something I only dream about.

I dream of going to school like my sister. Mama said going

to school in my country of Uganda isn't guaranteed like it is in America. The government doesn't pay for each child to attend school, so families have to use their own money. That means not all children in Uganda are able to attend school like they are in America. I feel education is a precious gift, and I'm jealous of all the children in America that go to school, even if their parents can't afford to pay the tuition. My parents can't afford my tuition, so education stays a dream for me. The Hope Institute helps Sarah by allowing her to go to school. Her sponsor even helped pay for her uniforms and supplies. Mama and Poppa were very grateful for that. I heard that children in America don't need to have a uniform, yet we must have two uniforms so we can have one to wear while the other one gets washed.

Mama and I are always sad when Sarah is getting ready to go to school since she goes to boarding school and is gone for many months at a time. I wouldn't complain if I could go to school, though. It would be an honor to be able to go to school and learn.

I tried to stop dreaming about what I knew I couldn't have, and instead stared at the bazungu from America. I found myself becoming more and more curious about them. Mama picked up a few more beads and some elastic and began making a new bracelet. I put the bazungu from America to the back of my mind and went to play with my brothers and sisters.

The next day at noon, when I was done eating my beans and rice, I saw the bazungu from America again. They had the same funny looking things with them, and I was even more curious than before. All of my brothers and sisters saw them too, and we all went to look at the new people with the strange black boxes hanging around their necks.

My sister, Sarah, had taught me some English so I walked over to a muzungu and shyly pointed at the black box hanging from her neck.

"What?" I asked. The woman looked at me with a smile.

"This? It's a camera! What's your name?" asked the woman. I wasn't sure of everything this muzungu said, but I thought she asked for my name.

"Joy," I told her.

The woman continued, "I'm Laurie, and it's very nice to meet you, Joy. How old are you?"

I wished Sarah had been with me, because I knew she would be able to understand. I worked hard to find the few

English words I had been taught. I wanted to talk to my new friend.

Then, out of the corner of my eye, I saw Sarah, who had learned English in school, and I knew she could help me! I waved for Sarah to come over and repeated Laurie's name. Laurie asked me for my age again.

"She does not know," Sarah answered for me. "Children born here do not have a record of when they were born. Most are born at home and no record is made. So we do not know."

"You don't know when your birthday is?" Laurie asked, quite surprised.

I shook my head and said, "No birthday!" I giggled, not quite understanding what this meant.

I saw Laurie looked surprised and could tell she wasn't sure what to say. A moment passed.

"Do you want to see what this does?" she asked, holding up the black box. My brothers and sisters jumped up and down excitedly, nodding their small heads. I started jumping too, even though I didn't exactly know why.

Laurie pointed the black box at me and pressed a little button that made a clicking sound. "Look," Laurie said, holding the black box out to me. I was so curious and excited when I saw my face on the tiny screen that I clapped my hands. I stared in amazement at the picture and at seeing myself on this black box. I could tell this box was very special to Laurie. I wanted to show her something special, too. So when my brothers and sisters were with the other people,

I grabbed her hand and pulled her to the backyard tree since I knew Mama wasn't there.

The first thing Laurie noticed was the tree branch where many strings of beads hung. Several stacks of magazines laid on the ground and various mats covered up the red dirt. Laurie watched me as I moved a giant stack of magazines toward the base of the tree. Then I climbed on the magazines and reached into a small hole inside the tree. As I climbed

down, I held a small package wrapped in newspaper.

"This," I said slowly, in the best English I knew, "is my sister's special bracelet." I carefully unfolded the package and handed the bracelet to Laurie.

"It's so pretty!" she said, taking the beautiful bracelet in her hands. There were many beads on the bracelet, all in different colors— red, blue, orange, yellow—and each bead was unique by its size, shape, color, and design. Laurie knew a lot of time and thought had been put into this special bracelet.

"For Sarah, from Mama," I tried to explain as Laurie continued looking at the bracelet. Right then, Sarah joined us. In my own language, I explained to Sarah what Laurie and I were doing. Sarah explained the story about the bracelet to Laurie.

"It was the first bracelet Mama ever made," Sarah said, "so it's really special to all of us. That's why we keep it in this secret part of the tree."

"Well that is very special," Laurie said smiling, handing the colorful bracelet back to me.

Mama called for Sarah to help her when, at the same moment, Gideon invited me to go play with a new ball he had just made. I have many brothers and sisters, so I always have playmates. Without thinking, I put the bracelet into my pocket. I smiled and waved good-bye to my new friend and followed Gideon out into the bright sun.

The next day when I got to the tree in the back to watch Mama work, I remembered I never put the special bracelet back! All at once, I realized I didn't know what happened to it. I ran back home and searched through my tattered clothes lying on the red dirt floor. Then, I realized the pocket I had put the bracelet in had a hole in it.

As soon as Mama stepped away, I quickly ran back to the tree. I stashed the wrapper in the cubbyhole, hoping Mama and Sarah wouldn't realize the special bracelet was missing. If I couldn't find the bracelet soon and if Mama told Poppa, my father wouldn't give me any food until it was found. I also knew I would have to go and get all the water, and I could barely stand that possibility. There was only one solu-tion—find the missing bracelet!

Determined, I started looking at the tree where I showed Laurie the bracelet. I got onto my hands and knees and looked all over the ground. When it didn't appear, I stepped out of the tree's cool shade. I looked all around where my brothers and sisters had played ball. I squinted, and in the distance I saw my new friend, Laurie, walking my way.

"Hi, Joy. You looking for something?" asked Laurie.

"Laurie! The special bracelet is not here!" I said, my voice was shaky, and my eyes began to water. I didn't want to cry, and Laurie could tell I was fighting back tears.

"Honey, it'll be okay," Laurie comforted me, rubbing my back. "I'll help you find it."

I stared at Laurie, and I was thrilled I understood Laurie's offer. Laurie would help me! I wasn't used to getting help from people I didn't know, especially muzungu. I thought Laurie was the nicest person I'd ever met.

"Webale, Nyabo," I said wrapping Laurie in a hug.

For a moment, Laurie was confused at what I had just said, but soon realized what I meant.

"You mean thank you? Well, you are very welcome, Joy," Laurie responded.

I was determined to find the bracelet. I couldn't even imagine what might happen to me if I didn't find the bracelet. Surely I would be in big, BIG trouble, especially with my father, and that was something I had never experienced. I saw Gideon get in trouble once, and I didn't want that to happen to me!

Laurie and I ran up and down the red dirt road I lived on, passing many potholes from the heavy rain and red brick huts with open windows. The bracelet still could not be found. We went everywhere we had gone the day before. I slowly started to realize I was never going to find it, and I would be in BIG trouble.

We reached the local church, and we both walked in. When Laurie and I saw Pastor Manasseh and his wife, Rose, Laurie asked them, "Have you seen a bracelet in here?"

"We have not, Laurie," Pastor Manasseh replied. "But feel free to look around."

Laurie and I did just that. We searched high and low, under every bench and in every corner. We even went up to the dirt platform, where the singers sang on Sunday mornings and the pastor preached, and looked behind every colorful banner. It was as if the bracelet had simply disappeared.

"If we find it, we'll let you know," Rose said. "We'll save it for you."

I was happy they would help me if they could. When our luck ran out in the church, Laurie pointed at the school-house down the road. This school was for the lucky children that go to day school. I had a friend who went there.

I shook my head, and mumbled, "Mbe," which Laurie

recognized as, "No." Laurie wondered why it couldn't be in the schoolhouse.

"It could be in there," Laurie said hopefully.

"No, no school. I no go there. But I want to. For Mama," I said, wanting to explain my wishes to go to school.

As Laurie listened closely, I could tell she was wondering why I couldn't attend school. She probably thought I had to help Mama make bracelets or stay with my younger siblings.

"Why can't you go to school?" Laurie finally asked, full of curiosity.

"No money," I replied sadly.

I didn't like to think about why I couldn't go to school. The only thing I liked to think about was how wonderful it would be to have my dream come true. I wanted to go to school like Sarah did so I could be educated and, in the future, educate others. My dream has always been to be a teacher. I know Mama wants that for me, too. She was sad the only thing holding me back was money. Mama made as many bracelets as she could, but the money had to go to support our family.

"Well," said Laurie, "I'm out of ideas where the bracelet might be. I'm really sorry, Joy."

"Mama mad," I said defeated, and we began walking down the road toward my home. I didn't want to talk, because I was fighting back tears. In my head, I was preparing a way to tell Mama that her special bracelet was gone forever. So far, I couldn't think of any excuse that would get me out of trouble.

When we stopped close to my home, I spotted something

colorful and shiny on the red dirt road, just a few feet away from where Laurie and I stood. I wasn't entirely sure what it was, but I had a feeling it was the answer to my problem. I ran to it and picked it up. I knew right away the shiny object was the special bracelet!

"You found it!" Laurie yelled to me. I couldn't help but jump up and down in excitement. I felt so relieved!

"That's great! Just in time too," Laurie said, nodding her head in the direction of my home. There stood Mama, with her arms crossed over her chest, staring at me with a smile on her face. Mama knew exactly the kind of trouble I had gotten myself into.

I smiled sweetly at Mama, knowing I had been caught but also saw that she didn't look too angry.

"Webale, Nyabo, Laurie," I said, as I stepped toward Mama.

Laurie smiled warmly at me and said, "You're welcome."

A week passed and I found myself talking a lot with Laurie. She was very nice, and I learned a lot from her. One day she brought a map and showed me where she lived and helped me find the city where I lived. I liked seeing where Laurie was from, the American state of Wisconsin, and Laurie showed me where Uganda was on the big continent of Africa. I found Lake Victoria on the map, and then Laurie showed me the city of Jinja. I tried to find my small village, but she said it wasn't on the map.

Sadly, Laurie's time to go home had come. On the day she left, Laurie shared some wonderful news with my family and me. I was going to be sponsored by the Hope Institute of Uganda. At first, I wasn't sure I understood what she was telling us, so I yelled for Sarah. Laurie explained everything to her.

"It means you're going to go to school, Joy!" Sarah said, in our native language. Sarah had a huge smile on her face. I could tell that Laurie was so happy to be able to help my family and me.

"Really?" I asked. I felt like my eyes were popping out of my head, not believing what was happening. I never thought I would be able to attend school. It was a miracle not only to my family but especially to me! I would finally be able to learn how to write and read and do all the things I never could before. I knew this was my first step toward becoming a teacher and being able to help others.

Laurie smiled, and I couldn't stop hugging her. I was so excited and happy!

"Webale, Nyabo! Webale, Nyabo! Webale, Nyabo!" I said over and over to Laurie.

She smiled and said, "You're welcome."

Finally, I would be able to attend school and one day, Mama says, provide for my own family. This was the one and only thing I had been wishing for since I was very young. I knew it was a precious gift. Most of my siblings and friends didn't go to school. I had been sure I would never be able to either.

It was hard to imagine being away from my family, but the idea of the Hope Institute paying my tuition, helping me get my own uniforms, my first pair of shoes, and school supplies to help me learn made me so happy. I couldn't stop smiling.

Not only did I avoid the disappointment from Mama, Poppa, and Sarah for losing their special bracelet, but I also found out that my dreams really could come true.

Thank you, friends from America that sponsor me. I thank God for you. I love you even though we have never met. One day I hope to meet you.

Hope
for **Joy**
Extras

Map of Uganda

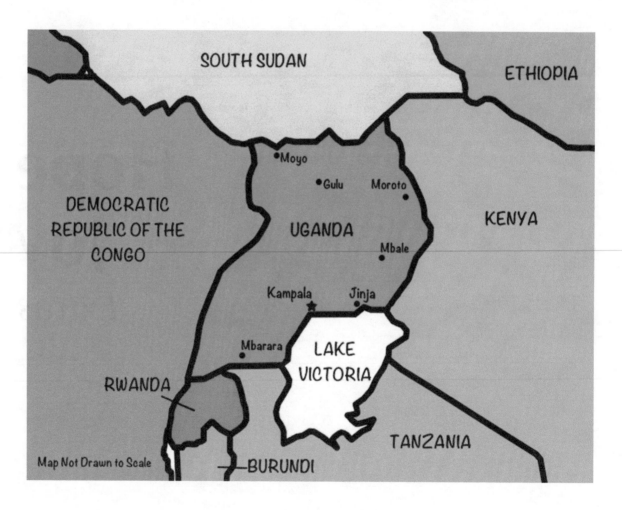

Map of Africa

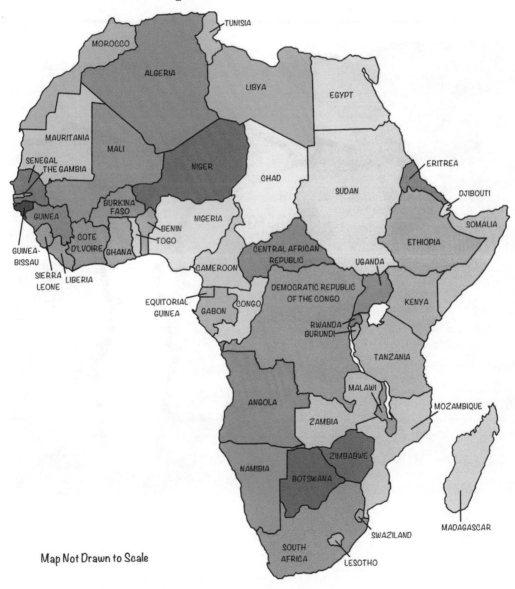

Map Not Drawn to Scale

Map of Wisconsin

Map of USA

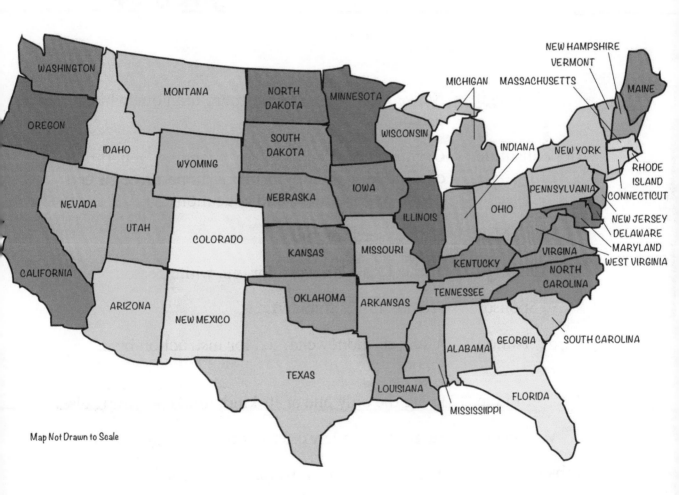

Map Not Drawn to Scale

Glossary of Terms

Bazungu	Native Ugandan word for more than one white person
Hope Institute of Uganda	Organization dedicated to changing generations one life at a time by bringing hope through economic opportunities and education
Mbe	Native word for "no"
Muzungu	Native Ugandan word for one white person
Sponsor	Provide funds (money)
Tuition	A sum of money charged for instruction by a school
Unique	Being the only one of its kind; unlike anything else
Volunteers	People who freely offer to do something
Webale, Nyabo	Native Ugandan word for "thank you"

A Special Thank You To

Sarah Miner for the original idea of the story and author of the initial drafts.

Sara Lynn Sanders for creating the beautiful illustrations.

Joy and Gideon Ngobi for their support and input.

The mentors and third grade children of Stuart Place School's Host program in Harlingen, TX for reading and providing input on the narrative.

Rose Manasseh, Ben and Venus Waiswa, and Sally Brandt for taking photos and being models for the illustrations.

Jean Olson, the project coordinator, for working seemingly endless hours to make this book a reality.

Acknowledgements

We wish to express our sincere gratitude to all our partners and supporters who have worked tirelessly on our behalf the past several years. Special thanks are extended to the people of our adopted hometown—Janesville, Wisconsin, USA—who believed in our vision when we first shared the need and opportunity for doing good deeds in our native Uganda; to our colleagues at Mercy Hospital, whose support has been unrelenting throughout this journey; to our church family at Janesville's Emmanuel Free Methodist Church and House of God who have shared their time, talent, treasures and prayers; and to those who have traveled alongside us even as a great recession was taking hold and hitting hard at home. We'd also like to thank our good friends at the Janesville Morning and Noon Rotary Clubs for helping and allowing us to get involved in our own community; the members of the Jinja Source of the Nile Rotary Club for their enduring and steadfast partnership; and to Pastor Manasseh at the Light and Life Church of Jinja, Uganda for his faithfulness and dependability. You are all so very special to us.

Having the opportunity to make a positive difference in the world has been one of the most rewarding experiences for us while living in the United States. When our friend and Rotary International Director, Mary Beth Growney Selene, learned of our plan to write and sell a book with the profits directly benefiting the people of Uganda, she told us "to dream big and always remember those who helped us along the way." With that in mind we've set a goal of selling one million books!

In closing, we thank you for buying and reading our book and encourage you to help the people of Uganda by helping to promote it, too. All proceeds will be used to make an immediate impact in educating a future young man or woman in Uganda.

Most sincerely,
Joy and Gideon Ngobi

About the Hope Institute

The Hope Institute of Uganda (HIU) is a 501(c)(3), nonprofit organization that has been registered in the state of Wisconsin since April 2008. HIU's vision is to improve the lives of Ugandan people who are being left behind. HIU's work focuses on leadership training, job creation, providing scholarships for youth and children in dire financial circumstances, and improving access to basic health care. Since the organization's conception, HIU has supported a group of ten bead makers that were trained by HIU, whose jewelry is sold under the title of Jinja Jewelry. These bead makers have created beautiful jewelry from recycled papers, and their work has mostly supported the missions of HIU. *Hope for Joy* is based off these bead makers' experiences and draws from the reality children face every day in Uganda.

Thank you to each and every person who has purchased *Hope for Joy*. Please know that your purchase will make an immediate impact on educating a future young man or woman in Uganda. With your purchase, you are fulfilling HIU's mission: "Changing generations, one life at a time." If you would like to know more about helping additional children get the education they deserve, please look at our website: *hopeinstituteuganda.org*, or give us a call at (608) 314-3950.

About the Creators

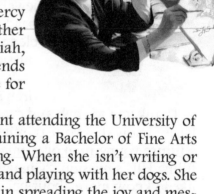

After seeing Jinja Jewelry at a craft show and falling in love with it, Jean Olson (project coordinator, top) volunteered to sell Jinja Jewelry and also visited Uganda and the children HIU supports. Jean is from Sun Prairie, Wisconsin and enjoys spending as much time as possible being a grandma to her four beautiful granddaughters: Taylor, Haley, Emily, and Sarah. She is married to Chuck Ashe who graciously supports her in her quest to help her Ugandan friends.

Joy Ngobi (founder, top right) was born and raised in Uganda but currently lives in Janesville, Wisconsin where she works as a staff anesthesiologist for Mercy Hospital. She is married to Gideon Ngobi and together they are raising three rambunctious sons: Jeremiah, Jacob, and Joshua. Joy enjoys meeting new friends and believes this book is a testimony for her love for people.

Sarah Miner (writer, center) is a college student attending the University of North Carolina Wilmington, working toward attaining a Bachelor of Fine Arts in Creative Writing and a certificate in publishing. When she isn't writing or reading, she enjoys spending time in the outdoors and playing with her dogs. She feels very privileged to have been an integral part in spreading the joy and message of the Hope Institute of Uganda.

Sara Lynn Sanders (illustrator, bottom left) is a mother of three, Laurel, James and Jason; a grandmother of three, Amanda, Brianna and Mitchell James; and a great-grandmother of Eli; as well as an illustrator and an author. She loves being able to support such a good cause and believes the education of these young men and women is a blessing in a world of struggle.